Thankful for Sweet Little You

By Tiffany Latino Gerlock
Illustrations by Camilla Galindo

Thankful for Sweet Little You

Copyright © 2023 Tiffany Latino Gerlock

Illustrations by artist Camilla Galindo, represented by Beehive Illustration.

All rights reserved. No part of this book may be reproduced in any form or by any electronic or mechanical means, including information storage and retrieval systems, without permission in writing from the copyright holder, except by reviewers, who may quote brief passages in a review.

ISBN: 9781088077535

This book was produced and published in partnership with
Blue Balloon Books, an imprint of Ballast Books.

www.blueballoonbooks.com

We love to partner with new authors and bring their books to life.
If you have an idea you know children would enjoy,
email us at info@blueballoonbooks.com.

To a dear Friend Enjoy!, Dino 2/23

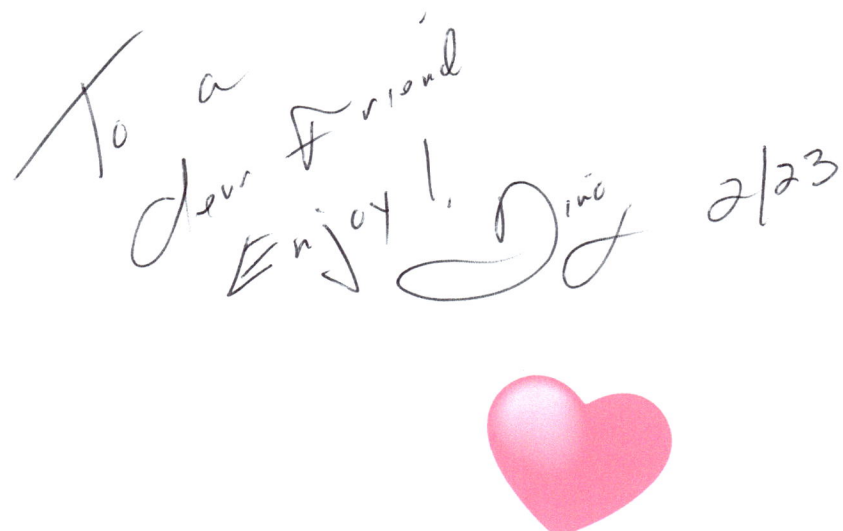

Dedication

For our sweet little Chase...
We love you and are thankful for you each day.

The sky is dark. The stars are bright.
It is time, sweet one, to say good night.

So, gather your toys and go upstairs and climb into bed to say your prayers.

Let us thank God for his gift of love that shines so bright in the stars above.

For animals that play on a warm, sunny day and the flowers that bloom and trees that sway.

Let us thank God for the birds that sing and the healthy gardens that grow in spring.

For raindrops and snowflakes that fall from the sky and our home that keeps us safe, snug, and dry.

And for cozy snuggles with teddy bear and a mommy's hug that shows she cares.

There are many blessings to thank God for: our friends and family whom we adore.

Now it's time, sweet one, to nestle in bed,
so I'll tuck you in and kiss your head.

I'm so thankful for sweet little YOU.

CPSIA information can be obtained
at www.ICGtesting.com
Printed in the USA
LVHW071525080123
736690LV00041B/573